Mystery Mob and the Abominable Snowman

Roger Hurn

Illustrated by

Stik

Rising Stars UK Ltd.
22 Grafton Street, London W1S 4EX
www.risingstars-uk.com

The right of Roger Hurn to be identified as the author of this work has been asserted by him in accordance with the Copyright, Design and Patents Act 1988.

Published 2007
Reprinted 2008

Cover design: Button plc
Illustrator: Stik, Bill Greenhead for Illustration
Text design and typesetting: Andy Wilson
Publisher: Gill Budgell
Publishing manager: Sasha Morton
Editor: Catherine Baker
Series consultant: Cliff Moon

British Library Cataloguing in Publication Data.
A CIP record for this book is available from the British Library

ISBN: 978-1-84680-226-3

Printed in the UK by CPI Bookmarque, Croydon, CR0 4TD

Contents

Meet the Mystery Mob 4

Chapter 1: A Winter Wonderland 7

Chapter 2: Tennis Rackets and Tea Trays 14

Chapter 3: Hangman's Hill 20

Chapter 4: Speed Thrills 25

Chapter 5: Crash Landings 31

Extras!

About the author 39

The snowman quiz 40

When I was a kid … 42

Adi's favourite snowman joke 43

Top tips for snowy weather 44

Five fantastic facts about snow 46

Snow lingo 47

Meet the Mystery Mob

Name:

FYI: Gummy hasn't got much brain – and even fewer teeth.

Loves: Soup.

Hates: Toffee chews.

Fact: The brightest thing about him is his shirt.

Name:

FYI: If Lee was any cooler he'd be a cucumber.

Loves: Hip-hop.

Hates: Hopscotch.

Fact: He has his own designer label (which he peeled off a tin).

Name:

Rob

FYI: Rob lives in his own world – he's just visiting planet Earth.

Loves: Daydreaming.

Hates: Nightmares.

Fact: Rob always does his homework – he just forgets to write it down.

Name:

Dwayne

FYI: Dwayne is smarter than a tree full of owls.

Loves: Anything complicated.

Hates: Join-the-dots books.

Fact: If he was any brighter you could use him as a floodlight at football matches.

Name: Chet

FYI: Chet is as brave as a lion with steel jaws.

Loves: Having adventures.

Hates: Knitting.

Fact: He's as tough as the chicken his granny cooks for his tea.

Name: Adi

FYI: Adi is as happy as a football fan with tickets to the big match.

Loves: Telling jokes.

Hates: Moaning minnies.

Fact: He knows more jokes than a jumbo joke book.

A Winter Wonderland

It's been snowing all night
and the Mystery Mob are out
making a giant snowman in the field
next to Witches Wood.

Chet Wow. Just look at our snowman.
It's brilliant.

Adi It is, but I bet you lot don't know
what you get if you cross
a snowman with a vampire.

Chet Okay. What do you get?

Adi Frostbite!

The Mystery Mob groan. They start to throw snowballs at Adi, to shut him up. Adi runs off, ducking and dodging the snowballs. Then suddenly he stops and stares at the ground.

Lee	What's up with Adi?
Dwayne	He looks scared stiff.
Gummy	It's so cold, maybe he's just *frozen* stiff.

Rob No, something's wrong.
Let's go and see what it is.

The boys dash over to where
Adi is standing. They skid to a standstill
next to him. Adi is staring at some
huge footprints in the snow.

Adi What do you think made these tracks?

Gummy I don't know, but whatever it is, it's huge!

Lee It's another mystery for the Mystery Mob to solve.

Dwayne In my Monster Book of Monsters it says only the Abominable Snowman has footprints this big.

Rob Is the Abominable Snowman real, then?

Dwayne Well, these prints are real. So what do you think made them?

Rob The Abominable Snowman?

Dwayne You said it.

Lee It looks like the monster's heading into town.

Rob Then we've got to stop him before he hurts anyone.

Lee We can phone the police.

Dwayne No we can't. The phone lines are down because of all this snow. It's up to us to do something.

Chet Come on then, Mystery Mob, there's no time to waste!

The boys try to follow the Abominable Snowman's tracks but the snow is too deep. It looks as if they'll have to give up. Then Dwayne has an idea.

Dwayne This is pants! We need to wear snowshoes if we're going to catch up with him.

Lee Great idea. Let's go and get some.

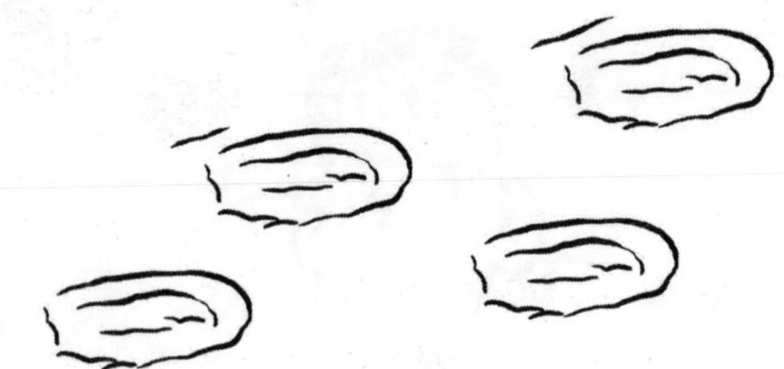

The boys dash back to their homes
to see if they can find any snowshoes.
They all agree to meet back at Witches
Wood as soon as they can.

Tennis Rackets and Tea Trays

Gummy and Dwayne are searching in Gummy's dad's shed for snowshoes.

Gummy It's no good. All I can find are these old tennis rackets.

Dwayne Excellent! They'll make brilliant snowshoes if we tie them on to our feet. Come on, let's do it!

Gummy But what if my dad needs them for playing tennis?

Dwayne Don't be daft. Nobody plays tennis in the snow. And anyway, the Abominable Snowman is on his way to trash the town! We've got to stop him – that's far more important than your dad playing tennis!

Gummy Too right it is. My dad can take up knitting if he wants something to do.

Gummy and Dwayne fix the tennis rackets to the bottom of their boots with some string. Then Dwayne spots something else.

Dwayne Oh yes – two tea trays! We'll take them with us. They'll be really useful.

Gummy Why? I thought we were going after the Abominable Snowman – not having a picnic.

Dwayne Duh. The Abominable Snowman has got a head start on us. So, if we're going to beat him into town and warn everyone of the danger, we'll need to move really quickly.

Gummy Isn't that why we're wearing snowshoes?

Dwayne Yes, but they won't be enough to do the trick. Now, here's my plan. We use the snowshoes to get to the top of Hangman's Hill, then we jump on these tea trays and speed down the slope.

Gummy I get it! The tea trays aren't really tea trays at all – they're sledges.

Dwayne Exactly! We'll zoom past the Snowman. Not even he will be able to travel that fast. By the time he finally arrives we'll be waiting for him with the cops.

Gummy Dwayne – you're a genius.

Dwayne I know – I just can't help it!

Hangman's Hill

Dwayne and Gummy set off to follow the footprints. There's no sign of the rest of the Mystery Mob.

Gummy Where are the others?

Dwayne I don't know, but we can't wait for them. We've wasted too much time as it is.

The boys struggle up Hangman's Hill. It's very hard going – even with their tennis racket snowshoes. They're out of breath and grumpy.

Gummy These tennis rackets are rubbish snowshoes.

Dwayne Stop moaning. We're catching up with the Abominable Snowman.

Gummy Says you. I still can't see him.

Dwayne Neither can I, but that's lucky.

Gummy Why is not being able to see the Abominable Snowman lucky?

Dwayne Because if we see him going up the slope, then he'll see us, and that will be very unlucky – for us!

Gummy Oh, right.

Dwayne We don't want to see him until we get to the top of the hill.

Gummy And we only want him to see us when we race past him on our tea tray sledges.

Dwayne You've got it.

Gummy I'm not dim, you know.

Dwayne No, of course not –
but you do have more brain cells
than teeth!

Speed Thrills

When they get to the top of Hangman's Hill, Dwayne and Gummy creep up to the edge and peer down the slope. They see the Abominable Snowman! He's about halfway down and heading towards the town.

Gummy There he is!

Dwayne Okay. We're just in time.
Let's jump on the tea trays
and zoom down the hill.
He'll never be able to catch us.
We'll be moving way too fast.

Gummy Er … how are we going to steer
the tea trays?

Dwayne They're not tea trays –
they're sledges.

Gummy Sorry. Er … how are we going to
steer the sledges?

Dwayne We don't need to steer them. We just point them at the bottom of the hill and they'll do the rest.

Gummy Are you sure about that?

Dwayne You said it yourself. I'm a genius. Trust me. Nothing can go wrong.

Gummy But what about the brakes?

Dwayne What about them?

Gummy We haven't got any.

Dwayne This is no time to be thinking about brakes. It's speed we want. Don't tell me you're scared. Are you a man or a mouse?

Gummy A man – but I do like cheese a lot.

The boys lie down flat on their backs
on the tea trays and push off.
Two seconds later they are speeding
faster than jet-powered bullets
down the icy slope.

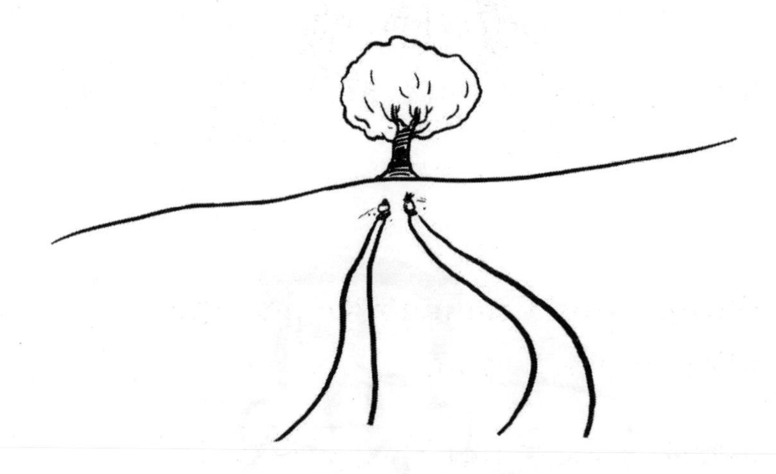

Crash Landings

Dwayne and Gummy race past the Abominable Snowman.

Dwayne (shouting) Yeeeeeeeeees!

Gummy (screaming) Nooooooooo!

The Abominable Snowman scratches his head in amazement. Then he covers his eyes with his paws. Dwayne and Gummy's tea trays are out of control. They are going to crash.

Dwayne (shouting) Look out! There's a big tree coming up fast.

Gummy (shouting) Trees can't move.

Dwayne No, but *we* can.

Gummy It's too late!

Dwayne (shouting) No it's not. Abandon tray!

In the nick of time the boys roll off their tea trays. The trays zoom on and crash into the tree. The tree shakes and dumps a great pile of snow from its branches on to Dwayne and Gummy.

Gummy Oh no. Here comes the Abominable Snowman.

Dwayne Don't move. He'll think we're two small snowmen.

Gummy But we don't have carrots for noses. And when he sees no noses, he'll smell a rat.

Dwayne Oh, take a chill pill, Gummy.

Gummy Why? That won't turn us into snowmen.

Dwayne (hissing) Please shut up or you'll give us away. Doh! Too late. He's looking right at us. We're history!

But to the boys' surprise the Abominable Snowman isn't a snowman at all. He's an actor wearing an Abominable Snowman costume.

Abominable Snowman

My car got stuck in a snowdrift – that's why I'm walking to town. I was just on my way to advertise my new movie, *Revenge of the Abominable Snowman.*

Gummy That's so cool.

Dwayne In fact, it's cooler than a loo seat at the North Pole.

Abominable Snowman

Hey – if you boys help me dig my car out, I'll give you free tickets to see the film!

Dwayne and Gummy

It's a deal!

So Dwayne and Gummy help the
Abominable Snowman dig his car out,
and he gives them free film tickets
for the whole Mystery Mob.

Dwayne Well, we've solved the mystery, and we can see the movie for free.

Gummy What do you think the rest of the Mystery Mob will say when we tell them?

Dwayne That there's *snow one* as smart as you and me!

About the author

Roger Hurn has:

 been an actor in 'The Exploding Trouser Company'

 played bass guitar in a rock band

- been given the title Malam Oga (wise teacher, big boss!) while on a storytelling trip to Africa.

Now he's a writer, and he hopes you like reading about the Mystery Mob as much as he likes writing about them.

The snowman quiz

Questions

1 What do you call a snowman on roller blades?

2 What kind of bikes do snowmen ride?

3 What cereal do snowmen eat for breakfast?

4 What do snowmen like to eat for lunch?

5 What does a snowman put on his icebergers?

6 What food do you get if you cross a snowman with a polar bear?

7 What do snowmen use to clean their teeth?

8 What do you call a snowman who uses too much toothpaste?

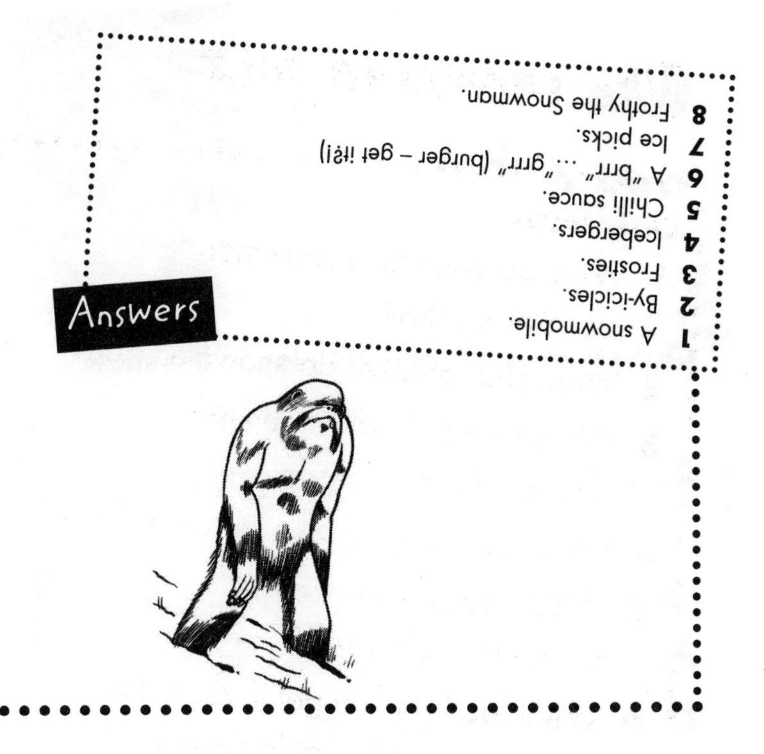

How did you score?

- If you got all eight snowman answers correct, then you are really chilled out!
- If you got six snowman answers correct, then you're cooler than a polar bear's nose.
- If you got fewer than four snowman answers correct, then you're in danger of melting!

When I was a kid

Question	Did you ever play in the snow when you were a kid?
Roger	Yes. I built a snowman but he didn't like me.
Question	How do you know?
Roger	He gave me the cold shoulder.
Question	Why was that?
Roger	Well, I took him to the snow ball but he wouldn't dance.
Question	Did your snowman wear a scarf?
Roger	No, but he did wear a hat.
Question	What kind of hat?
Roger	An ice cap. Er … I think I'd better melt away after that last joke.

Adi's favourite snowman joke

Top tips for snowy weather

If it's snowing hard outside – stay indoors. You can always go out in the snow when it's stopped.

If you think you're smart enough to survive in a blizzard, shine a torch into one ear. If the light shines out of your other ear – you're not.

When going out in the snow always wrap up warm and wear a hat, gloves, a scarf, woolly socks and boots or shoes with a good grip.

Never spit when you're facing a cold north wind – you could take your eye out!

Take care when throwing snowballs – they can hurt!

Rubbing sunscreen lotion on to your snowman will not stop it from melting.

Never stay in a snow house called an ig. It hasn't got a loo.

Five fantastic facts about snow

1 Snowflakes start as ice crystals
that are no bigger than a speck of dust.

2 Lots of people say that no two snowflakes
are the same. This isn't true,
but the chances of two snowflakes
being exactly alike are about
one million trillion to one!

3 If you melt ten centimetres of snow
you get one centimetre of water.
Just think how much snow you would need
to melt for a bath!

4 If the weather gets too cold it won't snow.

5 You can make snow with machines
called snow cannons.
But they cost so much
only big shots
can afford them.

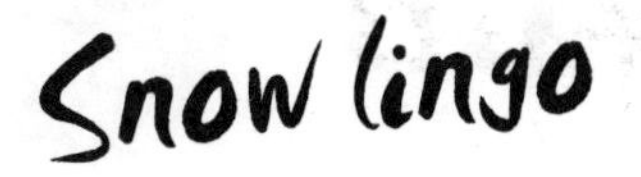

Blizzard A big snowstorm with really strong winds – not a type of big reptile.

Flurry Light snow that only falls for a little while. It's a flurry in a hurry.

Slush A messy mix of partly melted snow and ice. A slush puppy is a young dog that's just come in from playing in the snow.

Sleet Rain and snow mixed up together. Don't mix up sleet with a sheet or you'll have a very cold bed.

Snow Soft white crystals of ice that fall from clouds. If it snows when you're wearing swimming trunks then it's snow joke.